Four little penguins walked along

and fell

into a giant

hole!

There, inside that snowy pit, was a funny-shaped, snowy mound

with two stripy legs sticking out and flippers that made a sound.

"What a weird bird,"
said Penguin Peg.

"That's no bird!"
said Penguin Paul.

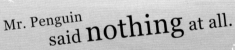

"Give it a poke!"
said Mrs. Penguin.

Mr. Penguin said nothing at all.

Then something small burst out and cried,
"I'm no bird. I'm Ed the ELF!
I fell out of Santa's Christmas sleigh –
now I've crashed and hurt myself!"

Mr. Penguin felt bad for Ed,
but he was also a bit confused.
He asked:

"What's an elf?

What's a sleigh?

What's a Santa?

What's a Christmas?

And are you bruised?"

"Oh, bloomin' baubles!" shouted Ed.
"You've never heard of Christmas Day?
I'll teach you how to celebrate
'til Santa returns in his sleigh!"

"First, some **sparkle** is what we need
to bring some **holiday glee**."

"Let's try to find some **twinkly** treats
we can hang on a **Christmas tree**."

But in the snow, it's hard to find
decorations to gleam and shine,

so what the penguins used instead

were **fish**

and some **boring,**

old twine!

Ed said, "Next, we'll get kind gifts
to show our friends that we care."

"But remember, they should be thoughtful,
not just fancy, sparkly, or rare."

The gift for Grandma Penguin
was cute, but it wasn't quite right;
it was much too wet,
much, MUCH too big,
and it gave her a little
fright!

Next, the penguins tried a carol
and though Ed sang with a smile,

Mr. Penguin's horrid, screeching squawks could be heard for miles and miles!

"I've ruined Christmas!" Mr. Penguin cried,

feeling rather sad.

Ed said, "I don't know what you **mean** –

it's the **most fun** I've **ever** had!"

"This Christmas may not be fancy,

but the spirit we have is right.

Let's laugh and sing and just be glad

we're together this Christmas night!"

But then, Ed's golden pocket watch struck twelve with a jingly chime.

"Oh, no!

The sleigh is almost here and I haven't made a sign!"

Mr. Penguin's family knew what to do; they had thought of the perfect gift!

They called all their penguin friends to make a sign in the snowdrift . . .

Santa flew over in his sleigh and from way up high, he could see some writing in the snow that said . . .

SANTA, RESCUE

As Santa landed with a THUD,

he cried out, "Well, what a sight!

I'll spend the rest of Christmas here –

it's the perfect end to my night!"

They celebrated together,

then when it was time to say goodbye,

Ed promised that next Christmas . . .

. . . he would be sure to drop by!